For my daughter, Polly,
who loves mice
—J. D.

For Bernadette, Jennifer,
and Christopher
—M. M.

First published 1990 by Methuen Children's Books

Text copyright © 1990 by Joyce Dunbar
Illustrations copyright © 1990 by Maria Majewska

Library of Congress Cataloging-in-Publication Data
Dunbar, Joyce.
Ten little mice/written by Joyce Dunbar; illustrated by
Maria Majewska.
p. cm.
"Gulliver Books."
Summary: Follows the activities of ten little mice as, one by one,
they scurry home to their nest.
[1. Mice—Fiction. 2. Counting.] I. Majewska, Maria, ill.
II. Title. III. Title: 10 little mice.
PZ7.D8944Te 1990
[E]—dc20 89-36463
ISBN 0-15-200601-X

ISBN 0-15-200770-9 pb
ISBN 0-15-284614-X oversize pb

First U.S. edition 1990

C E G I K L J H F D

Printed in Hong Kong

Ten Little Mice

Ten Little Mice

Written by Joyce Dunbar

Illustrated by Maria Majewska

GULLIVER BOOKS • HARCOURT, INC.

San Diego   New York   London

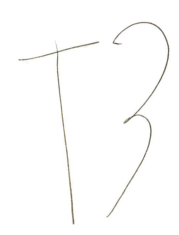

Ten little mice were grooming themselves,
Their ears, their tails, their whiskers.
"Now I'm so very clean," said one,
"I'm going-going home to my cozy nest."

Nine little mice in a row of beans
Were digging and scratching for seeds.
One was scared when a robin got mad,
So he scurry-scurried home to his cozy nest.

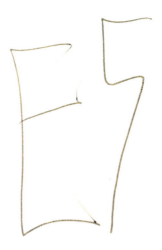

Eight little mice in a barley field
Were climbing from stalk to stalk.
One saw the tail of a prowling cat,
So he ran-ran home to his cozy nest.

Seven little mice in an underground tunnel
Were snooping and sniffing and spying.
One saw a badger's long striped snout,
So he rush-rushed home to his cozy nest.

Six little mice found a wild bees' nest
And dipped all their paws in the honey.
One little mouse heard an angry buzz,
So he skip-skipped home to his cozy nest.

F4

Five little mice gnawing hazelnuts
Were chomping and champing and chewing.
One little mouse felt so very full,
That he stagger-staggered home to his cozy nest.

Four little mice by a cool dark pool
Were splishing and splashing and sliding.
One fell in, and soaked to the skin,
He slip-slopped home to his cozy nest.

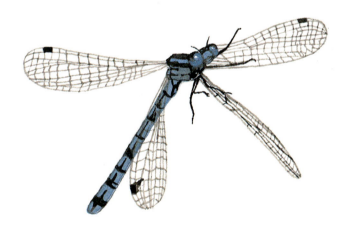

Three little mice on an old tree stump
Were twitching their noses at sheep.
One found a fluffy bit of wool and said,
"This is fine-fine-fine for my cozy nest."

Two little mice in the dried brown leaves
Frolicked and frisked just for fun.
One heard the swoop and the hoot of an owl,
So he dash-dashed home to his cozy nest.

One little mouse in a thunderstorm
Saw the crick-crack-crick of the lightning.
"I've had enough for tonight," he said.
So he hurry-hurried home to his cozy nest.

Ten little mice safe home at last
Were snuffling and sniffling and snoring.
Each had a dream of daring deeds
As they slept-slept sound in their cozy nest.